Costas Andreou

The Nose Family: Scruffy's Lucky Day

Nightingale Books

NIGHTINGALE PAPERBACK

© Copyright 2022
Costas Andreou

A CIP catalogue record for this title is
available from the British Library.
ISBN 978-1-83875-622-2

Nightingale Books is an imprint of
Pegasus Elliot MacKenzie Publishers Ltd.
www.pegasuspublishers.com

First Published in 2022

Nightingale Books
Sheraton House Castle Park
Cambridge England

Printed & Bound in Great Britain

Dedication

to George Andreou, Antony Andreou, & Cary Kikis

Author message

Hi everyone!

There is a little yellow bird on each illustration that must be found.

Some are easy, and some are hard. Shout out once you see it.

Once not so long ago, the noses were all happy and everyone in nose town was busy.

Nothing seemed odd or out of place, but the town and all the different noses were all about to be surprised.

Mrs Nose was using the golden pen for some shopping, as she would most weeks.

Now all the noses in town were starting to nose around their house, wondering why they would never see Mrs Nose or her family in the shops buying anything.

One day Mrs Nose got a phone call while she was writing the weekly shopping list with the golden pen.

When the call was over, she completely forgot to put the golden pen back in the secret place she hid it because she would only use it once a week.

She left the house to go and see a friend.

After a few days Mr Nose found the pen. Not knowing what it could do, he took it with him to work in the library.

He did not know that it was magic, but he was sure he needed a pen that day.

At the end of the day Mr Nose finished work and left the pen on his desk. He didn't even use it once.

The next day, Mini Nose asked Mrs Nose to get her some paint canvas and paper, so Mrs Nose went to get the golden pen but couldn't find it.

That's when Mrs Nose started to get really worried.

She didn't know where to look, so she looked everywhere

(even in the loo).

At the same time in the library, a little nose called Scruffy
came across the golden pen while asking for a book, and thought he
could use it.

The Scruffy family lived on the edge of Nose town and was one of the oldest families in Nose town.

There was Scruffy, his mum Mrs Scruff, his dad Mr Scruff, his grandparents and their best friend, Scratchy the pooch.

Scratchy was a very old dog that would go walkies alone and get a little confused.

Sometimes he would come home after an hour or a day and sometimes even after a week.

There were even times where he didn't even realise that he had gone anywhere at all.

Most of the noses in and around Nose town have seen Scratchy the pooch at one time or another, or at least smelt him as he had a strong smell of soggy wet socks wherever he went.

All the noses would get irritated with Scruffy's dad because Mr Scruff would drive around Nose town once a day and put his extra rubbish in everyone elses bins.

Mr Scruff liked to collect things, and he had lots of space because the Scruffy family lived on the edge of town, but their house was small and old.

He would try to keep almost everything he collected, but the few things he didn't want would be spread around the bins in town.

CASTLE SCRUFF

On a day like any other, Scruffy Nose was getting ready for school and almost forgot his homework.

It was a simple task, he had to draw a picture of where he would like to live most of all.

Scruffy Nose found an old piece of paper, and without thinking, he used the golden pen for the first time to draw a castle. As he thought his teacher might not be sure what it was, he wrote castle under the picture.

Then he left the pen on his bed and ran to school.

He was always a bit late because he lived on the edge of town. He decided to try running to make sure he was on time.

He was in such a terrible hurry that his homework fell from one of the many holes in his pockets without him even noticing.

He arrived at school late, as he always did, and his teacher asked everyone to hand in their homework.

He could not find it anywhere!

He was so sure he did his homework, and he was very upset when the teacher asked him to stay after school.

Once the teacher let him go home, all the other children had already gone, and he was the last person to leave school, again.

This was not the first time this had happened.

On his way home he was looking at all the beautiful houses, dreaming and wishing his home was as clean and tidy as them.

(and maybe just a little bit bigger too, as his house was the smallest in Nose town.)

When Scruffy Nose came home a little late, just like every other day, his mother Mrs Scruffy warmed up his supper and he sat alone to eat it, still upset about his homework.

Once he finished, he cleared his plate and went off to bed.

He was still a little bit sad, but the next morning would surprise him and his whole family...

As he opened his eyes, he looked around and saw he wasn't in his tiny room anymore!

Scruffy's room had turned into the most amazing bedroom he could ever imagine. He had to roll over and over 5 times just to get out of bed!

His family were all awake and running around, opening all the doors looking for the loo.

Once they found the most important room (the bathroom), all of Scruffy's family got together and decided on a plan to look for the kitchen.

18

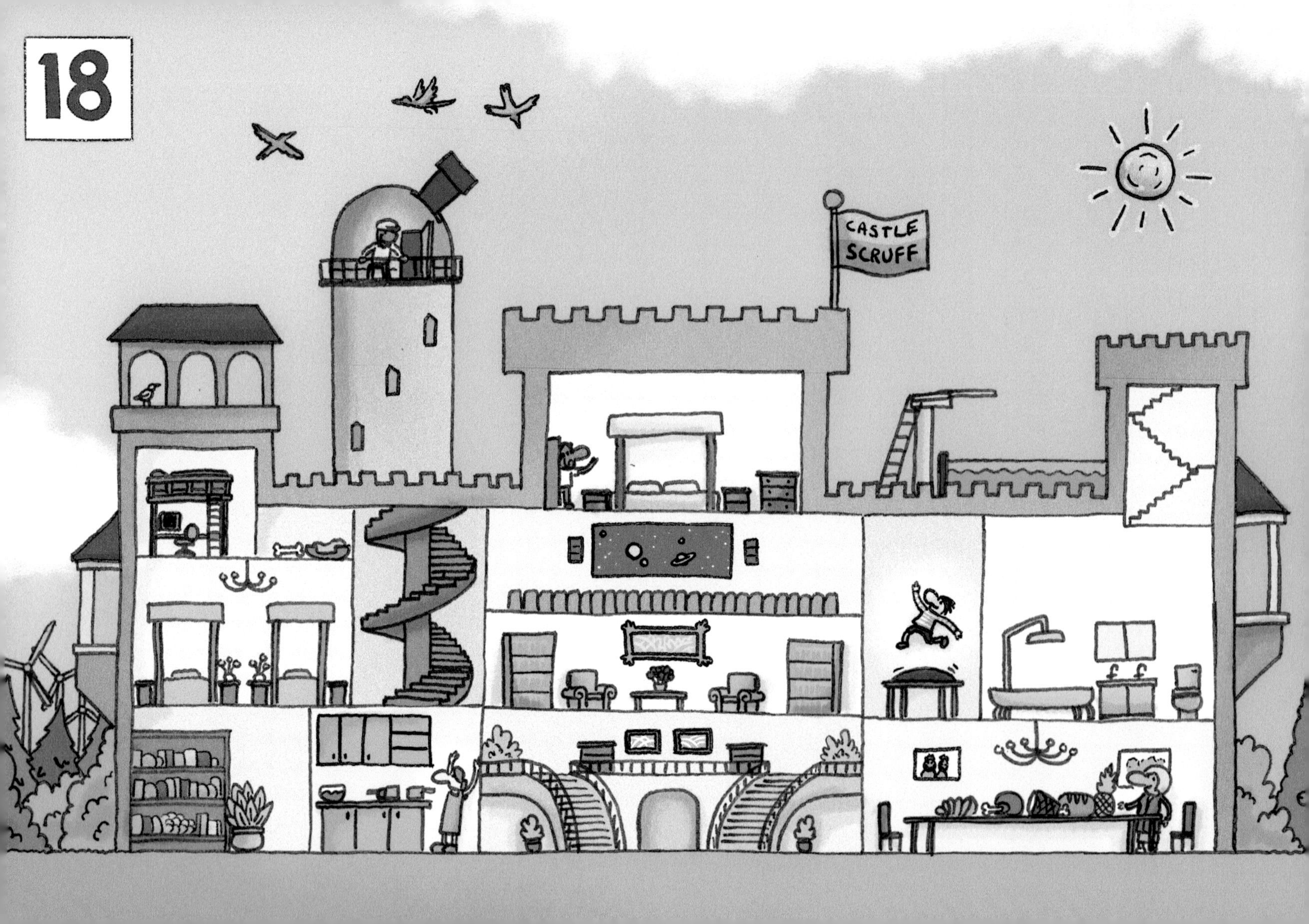

Scruffy didn't go to school that day. He stayed to explore the castle with his family.

They looked upstairs and downstairs, into what must have been over 100 rooms.

Slowly all the rooms were opened, and they even found the way out!

The whole of the Scruffy family stood outside really confused.

They couldn't believe that their tiny little house had turned into the most beautiful castle, with a draw bridge and moat!

The whole family was amazed, but decided it was too grand to live in. Maybe they could give it to the Mayor!

All of the Scruffy family went to see the Mayor of Nose town to explain, and to offer the castle to him.

The Mayor of Nose town lived in a lovely house right in the middle of town near the school.

The mayor wouldn't and couldn't believe the Scruffy family. He knew their house was small and full of junk, not a grand castle. So the Mayor of Nose town decided to go see for himself, as he thought the Scruffy family were trying to play a trick on him.

Once they arrived at the castle there was a large crowd of noses outside, confused and amazed by the beautiful castle.

The mayor was so impressed on how big and beautiful it was, he agreed to move in!

He decided to offer the Scruffy family his house because they didn't want to stay in the castle.

The Scruffy family were so happy. Scruffy was never late for school again, and Mr Scruff completely stopped collecting old junk!

Instead, Mr Scruff got a job putting up signs on all the doors so the mayor would never get lost.